LAURENT DE BRUNHOFF

BABAR'S
GUIDE TO PARIS

ABRAMS BOOKS FOR YOUNG READERS
NEW YORK

The illustrations in this book were made with watercolor on paper.

Cataloging-in-Publication Data has been applied for and may be
obtained from the Library of Congress.

ISBN: 978-1-4197-2289-9

Printed and bound in China
10 9 8 7 6 5 4 3 2 1

Abrams Books for Young Readers are available at special discounts when
purchased in quantity for premiums and promotions as well as fundraising
or educational use. Special editions can also be created to specification.
For details, contact specialsales@abramsbooks.com or the address below.

ABRAMS The Art of Books
115 West 18th Street, New York, NY 10011
abramsbooks.com

TO ALISON LURIE

Babar's youngest daughter, Isabelle, is going to Paris. Babar has been there often. It is one of his favorite cities. Before she leaves, he tells her how to enjoy it.

First, he says, you must go to a *café*.
Order anything. You can sit as long
as you like. Read a book or just watch
the world go by.

The *café* is the theater of Paris, where you are both actor and spectator.

Each *café* is different. Café de Flore and Deux Magots are right next door to each other. Celeste frequents the Flore, while Cousin Arthur prefers Deux Magots.

The *cafés* are full day and night. There is never a wrong time to stop for a coffee, a *citron pressé*, or an ice cream.

If you stand at the bar, it costs less.

Have dinner at a *brasserie*. This is a lively restaurant where you can eat just about anything you want. Some of my favorites are La Coupole, Balzar, Le Vaudeville, and Bofinger.

The seafood platters are amazing!

Best of all, you can bring your dog!

Find your own favorite restaurant and go there often. Then the waiters will greet you as a friend.

Despite its good reputation, the weather in Paris can be rainy, chilly, and windy.

Take your down or leather jacket and a warm wool scarf. If you forget something, don't worry. There are many *chic* stores in Paris, and shopping there is fun.

Apartment houses have coded number panels instead of doormen at the outer door. You must know a friend's code as well as her address.

The elevator is likely to be small.

Paris has many thriving bookstores. You can also find

used books, posters, and prints at stalls along the Seine.

Take the subway, called the Métro.

When the train starts, grab a pole and hold on tight!

Go to museums, especially the Louvre,
which you enter through a glass pyramid.

You will see many
strange and beautiful
things inside.

See Monet's paintings of water lilies at
the Orangerie museum.

Take *a bateau mouche* and see Paris from the river. Admire the Eiffel Tower from every angle.

Exchange ideas with a friend in the Luxembourg Gardens.

Live like a Parisian. Enjoy food and conversation and every scrap of good weather you get. Walk everywhere. Walk as much as you can.

There will be a
surprise on every
block—a lion . . .

an artist . . .

. . . maybe children learning anatomy from statues!

You might see a street market in the morning,
which will have disappeared by the afternoon.

There will always be a park nearby to explore . . .

. . . or to relax in.

At night, go to the theater or the opera.

Next morning, laze on the quays of the Seine. Love Paris, as we all do. Dream about living in Paris, as we all have.

See the great world and treasure every
bit of it, darling child. But at the end of
your journey, come back to your family in
Celesteville and let us welcome you home.